EMMA PEROR'S NEW CLOTHES

BY ISABEL THOMAS

ILLUSTRATED BY ERICA JANE WATERS

Curious Fox

This story is based on The Emperor's New Clothes, a fairy tale written by Hans Christian Andersen in 1837. The original story is about an emperor who spends all his time thinking about new clothes. One day, two crooks arrive in town. They pretend to be weavers of magnificent cloth that becomes invisible to anyone who is stupid or not good enough at his or her job. The emperor orders a costume from them and plans a procession through the city to show it off.

The crooks take lots of money and expensive materials from the emperor, but only pretend to weave. Two trusted officials are sent to check on the costume. They don't want to look foolish, so they pretend to see fabric on the empty looms. The emperor is also afraid to say anything, and the crooks pretend to dress him for the procession.

As the emperor walks through the streets, the whole city pretends to see the emperor's new clothes. Nobody wants to look foolish. Then a little child cries out, "But he doesn't have anything on!" Soon the whole town is laughing at the foolish and vain emperor.

First published in 2015 by Curious Fox,
an imprint of Capstone Global Library Limited,
264 Banbury Road, Oxford, OX2 7DY
Registered company number: 6695582

www.curious-fox.com

Illustrations by Erica Jane Waters

ISBN 978 1 782 02315 9
19 18 17 16 15
10 9 8 7 6 5 4 3 2 1

A CIP catalogue for this book is available from the British Library.

Printed and bound in China.

For Hellé and Zöe

CAST OF CHARACTERS

Emma
Peror

Trixie
Tailor

Dee

Tiny child

Ballet
teacher

Dom

Emma Peror was the ballet class terror. She would do anything to be the best dancer.

Emma was even horrid to her friends, but no one dared to tell the teacher.

Emma was sure she'd be the star of the big ballet show. Then a new girl joined the class.

"This is Trixie Tailor," said the teacher. "Her mum is a famous ballet dancer."

"What pretty hair she has," said Dee.

"And what an amazing tutu," said Dom.

Emma said nothing, but her face turned green.

Emma was jealous.
She distracted Trixie
as she danced...

... bumped her off
balance

... and tripped her
every time she twirled.

At the end of the class, Emma hissed something in Trixie's ear.
Hand over that tutu!

"I've got a better tutu at home," said Trixie. "It's so magical, silly people and bad ballet dancers can't even see it!"

"I want to wear THAT in the ballet show," said Emma.

"No problem," smiled Trixie.

Emma told the whole town about
the magical tutu.

"Bad ballet dancers can't even
see it!" she boasted.

"Have you seen the tutu?" asked Dee.

Suddenly, Emma felt a teeny bit worried.

"Go and see Trixie," Emma snapped.
"Make sure the tutu is ready."

Ten minutes later, Trixie pretended to show the magical tutu to Dee and Dom.

"Look at the pretty patterns and the sparkling skirts," she said.

Dee and Dom stared and stared.

They didn't want to look silly, so they said nothing at all.

Back at the playground,
Emma was eating an ice
cream she had taken from
a toddler.

"Well?" she snapped.

"The tutu is beautiful," said Dee.

"Spellbinding," said Dom.

Emma giggled with glee. She would be the best dressed dancer on stage.

On the day of the show, Trixie pretended to give Emma the magical tutu.

But Emma could see nothing at all!

She didn't want to look silly, so all she said was "Get out of my way while I put it on!"

The whole town was waiting for the show to begin.
A spotlight lit up the curtains...

... and out danced
Emma, wearing
nothing but a vest and
enormous, spotty pants!

Nobody dared to speak.

Then a child in the front row cried out, "Look at that silly girl. She hasn't got anything on!"

The audience chuckled.

The other dancers giggled.

Soon everyone was roaring with laughter.

Suddenly, Emma felt very silly indeed. She stomped off stage in the tutu that wasn't there.

"We can all be stars of the show now," said Trixie, and the rest of the dancers swished, swirled and twirled in the best ballet show the town had ever seen.